E
Ca

Carlson, Nancy

Louanne Pig in the
perfect family

DATE DUE

SEP. 2 1 1989	JUL. 0 4 1995	AUG. 0 6 1997
MAR. 3 1 1990	OCT. 0 5 1995	APR 0 7 1998
MAY 0 7 1990	OCT. 2 7 1995	MAY 1 1 1998
AUG. 2 9 1990	APR. 0 6 1996	JUL 2 0 1999
SEP. 2 8 1991	MAY 0 4 1996	AUG 2 4 2000
NOV. 1 0 1992	JUN. 2 5 1996	FEB 2 6 2001
JUL. 0 2 1993	JUN 2 9 1996	JUN 2 9 2001
AUG. 0 6 1993	JUL. 0 9 1996	SEP 1 3 2001
AUG. 2 7 1993	JAN. 2 4 1997	AUG 0 2 2002
OCT. 0 9 1993	JUN. 3 0 1997	OCT 3 0 2007
NOV. 1 1 1993	JUL. 0 4 1997	NOV 2 0 2008
AUG. 2 2 1994	AUG. 0 5 1997	

THE PERFECT FAMILY

· *Louanne Pig in* ·

THE PERFECT FAMILY

Nancy Carlson

Carolrhoda Books, Inc. ◆ **Minneapolis**

LIBRARY OF CONGRESS CATALOGING-IN-PUBLICATION DATA

Carlson, Nancy L.
 Louanne Pig in the perfect family.

 Title on added t.p.: The perfect family.
 Summary: Louanne thinks she wants to be part of a
big family until she spends a weekend with her friend
George and his five sisters and four brothers.
 1. Children's stories, American. [1. Brothers and
sisters — Fiction. 2. Family life — Fiction] I. Title.
II. Title: Perfect family.
PZ7.C21665Lkh   1985   [E]   85-4123
ISBN 0-87614-280-3

 2   3   4   5   6   7   8   9   10   94   93   92   91   90   89   88   87   86

To my perfect family, Barry and Kelly

Louanne lived with her mother and her
father. George lived next door with his mother
and his father and his five sisters and his
four brothers. There was never a dull moment
in *their* yard.

"Don't you think ten kids make a perfect family?" Louanne asked her mom.

"You and Daddy are the perfect family for me," said Mom.

"Didn't you ever think about adopting some more kids?" Louanne asked her dad.

"Nope," said Dad. "You're all I can handle."

Then one night Mom said, "My office just called. I have to fly to Dallas in the morning, and this is Daddy's fishing weekend. How would you like to spend the weekend at George's house?"

"Would I ever!" said Louanne.

On Friday afternoon Louanne packed: two nice outfits, a nightgown, a good book, her toothbrush and toothpaste, a towel, and a large bag of jellybeans.

"Off I go!" she told her parents.

"I'm afraid you'll have to share a bedroom
with the girls," George's mother told Louanne.
"Oh, that will be wonderful!" said Louanne.
"I've never shared a room before."

George took Louanne upstairs so she could leave her suitcase in her room. Then they went outside to play.

As they ran outside, Louanne slipped on a
roller skate and fell down.

"You have to watch your step around here," said George. "Hal leaves his stuff all over the place."

In the middle of a game of catch, Louanne felt her shirt getting wet.

"Is it raining?" she asked.

"No, it's Tony," said George. "He got a new squirt gun this morning. Just ignore him and he'll go away."

Suddenly a loud bell began to clang.

"Dinner!" yelled George, and Louanne was
left behind in a cloud of dust.

By the time she made it to the table,
everyone else was already there.

"Hey, Margaret, pass on the corn before
you've taken it all!" Tony was yelling.

"Tony," wailed Harry, "you took the last
carrot!"

"Pass the squash!" yelled Hal.

"Please pass the squash," said his mother.

"ME FIRST!" yelled Hal.

Dinner at my house is never like this, thought Louanne.

Later Louanne went upstairs to unpack. Her clothes were strewn all over the room, and her bag of jellybeans was nearly empty.

"It must have been Nancy," said George. "She gets into everything. She's too little to know better."

That night Louanne made an even worse
discovery: Eleanor snored.

The next morning Louanne didn't feel too
rested. Maybe a cold shower will wake me up,
she thought, but she was last in line for the
bathroom.

At breakfast George's mother announced a picnic in the park. Oh, good, thought Louanne. Maybe George and I can sneak away and play by ourselves.

But George had to help keep an eye on
the little kids,

and the potato salad wasn't the way Louanne's
mother made it, either.

That evening Louanne tried to find a quiet
corner where she could read, but it was no use.

"Doesn't all this noise all the time drive you crazy?" she asked George.

George looked surprised. "I like it this way," he said.

Sunday morning Louanne packed her suitcase again. As soon as she saw her parents
drive up, she rushed home.

"Boy, am I glad to see you!" said Louanne.

"How was your weekend?" Mom asked. "Was it fun being part of a big family?"

"Oh," said Louanne, "a big family is just great...

…for George. But you and Daddy are the perfect family for me. Do we have any more jellybeans?"